Bedtime for Dragons

Written By
Elizabeth Bell

Illustrated By
Kevin Harrell

BRIT BOOKS
Chandler, Arizona

BEDTIME FOR DRAGONS

Published by:

Brit Books

Email: britwalker17@gmail.com

Brittney Walker, Publisher

Yvonne Rose/Quality Press.info, Book Packager

Illustrator: Kevin Harrell

Copyright © 2019 by Brittney Walker

ISBN: 978-0-578-44318-8

Library of Congress Control Number: 2019933509

DEDICATION

To my little reptilian pets, Geiko (RIP) and Dragon. Without them, this book would not exist.

ACKNOWLEDGEMENTS

I would like to give a special thanks to my friend, Kevin Ares, for his support and generosity. To my cousin, Kevin Harrell, I owe a big thank you for his beautiful illustrations and for bringing my characters to life. And to my parents who fostered my love of the arts since I was a child – love always, thank you.

Up in the mountains

On the highest peak,

There were two little dragons

Who were desperately trying not to sleep.

They wanted to play

Under the moon in the sky,

And fly to the tops of the trees

With their wings spread out wide.

But Mama Dragon tucked them in

With stern warnings to stay in bed,

With a kiss and a "sleep tight"

And the blankets pulled up to their heads.

But the little dragons could not rest

And "sleep tight" in their beds,

When big adventures to be had

Lay right outside instead.

But they knew there was no escape

For Mama Dragon was too wise,

So against their hopes and wishes

The little dragons shut their eyes.

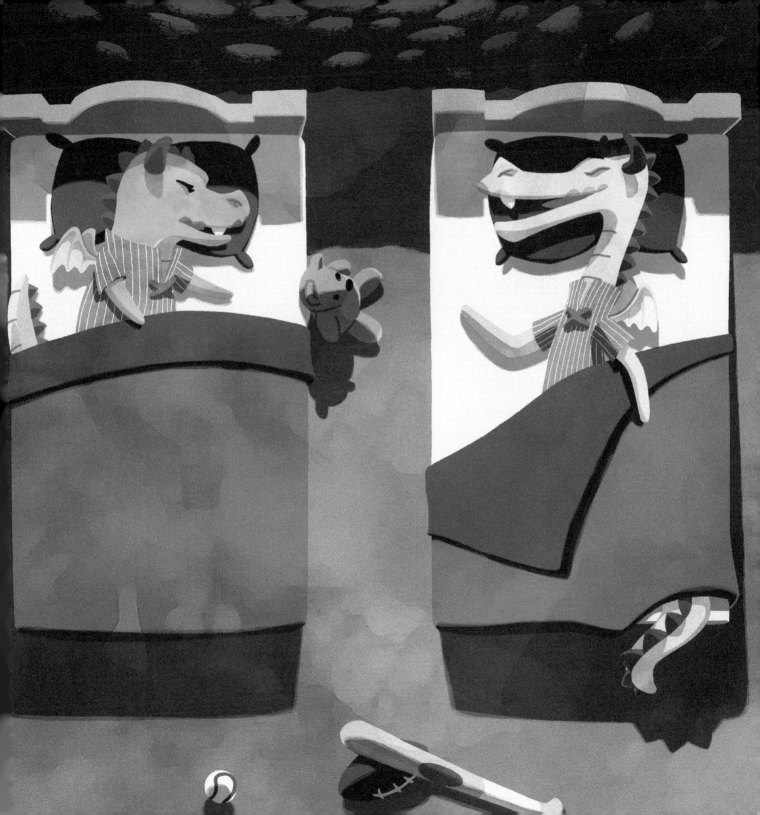

In the little dragons' heads

Danced adventures far and wide,

As they lay tucked in their beds

Their dreams took them outside.

The little yellow dragon dreamt

He was flying in the sky

Above oceans, mountains, and rivers

Until he was really quite up high.

He flew until he tired

And could not fly anymore,

So slowly he came to rest

In front of a big castle door.

He dreamt he saved the castle

From fierce and terrible knights,

They were so afraid of him

He did not even have to fight!

The little yellow dragon laughed

In his castle he was King!

This was more fun than playing outside;

In his dreams, he could be anything!

The little yellow dragon slept,

But he was not dreaming alone

For the little pink dragon

Was having adventures of her own.

She dreamt she was climbing

Up a mountaintop in the clouds.

When she came across a party

Where grown-up dragons were not allowed.

The party had lots of games,

Even music and cartoons.

It had the pink dragon's favorite thing,

The MOST important thing – food!

The little dragon ate all she could

From the ground to the mountain tip.

She could hardly believe her eyes,

"Look at all the candy, cookies, and chips!"

She ate all the treats and snacks

Playing games and flying around.

She flew to the mountaintop to say,

"This is the best party in all of town!"

The little dragons slept all night

With castles and parties in their heads.

Who needs to go outside at all! they thought,

We can have adventures without leaving our beds!

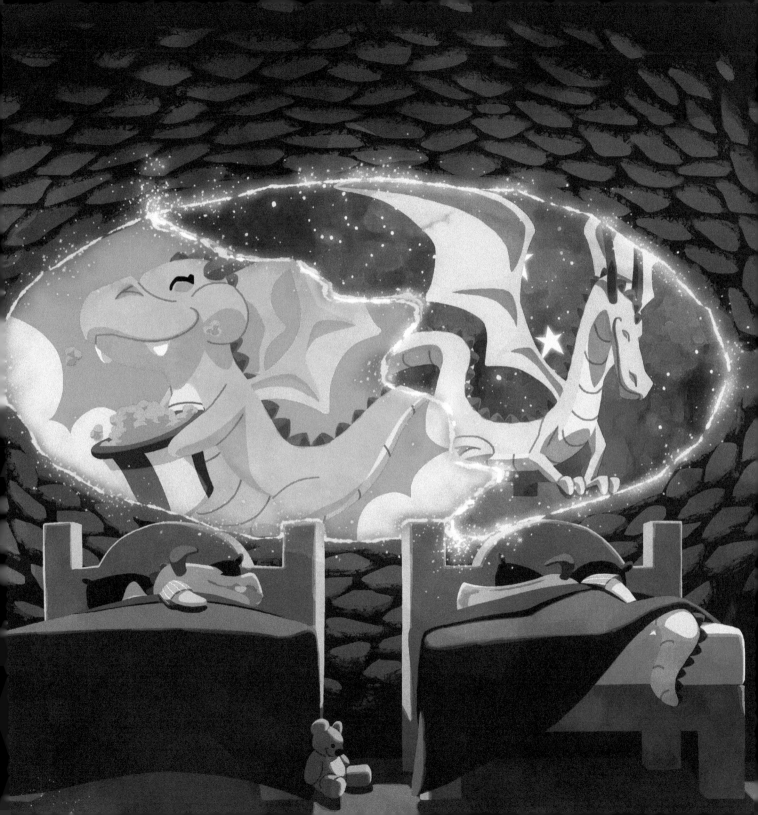

When the dragons woke in the morning

And Mama took them out to play,

They soon found that the true fun

Was in their dreams – where they ought to have stayed.

And as they flew outside

Playing games with their friends,

The little ones could not wait

Until it was bedtime for dragons again.

ABOUT THE AUTHOR

Elizabeth Bell is a Chicago-born writer of short stories, poetry, and children's books. She has been writing since the age of nine. Although a music major in college, she continued to express herself in her free time through the written word, particularly focused on love poems. Her first published work, *Bedtime for Dragons* is an adventure into her creative writing style. She currently resides in Arizona with her leopard gecko, Dragon, who is the inspiration for this book.

ABOUT THE ILLUSTRATOR

Kevin Harrell is a self-taught artist, who fell in love with creating at a very young age. He was born and raised on the south side of Chicago, and greater Chicagoland area throughout his formative years. The rich history and culture of Chicago has heavily influenced his passion for art. He grabs inspiration from masters of the art world, domestic and abroad - artists such as Hayao Miyazaki, Kim Jung Gi, LeSean Thomas, and others. *Bedtime for Dragons* is his second venture into children's book illustration. He also worked on a popular webcomics series called *Albert the Alien*. What Kevin aims to do with his art is warm the hearts and inspire the creativity of budding young minds all over the world.

CPSIA information can be obtained
at www.ICGtesting.com
Printed in the USA
LVHW070152010319
609163LV00011B/33/P